THE TREE
HOUSE

André Deutsch

THE TREE HOUSE

Story and pictures by
Joanna Stubbs

On the hilltop stood a tree which, each spring, looked like a leafy lighthouse covered with lights. It was a chestnut tree. And that chestnut tree had a secret.

In summertime birds sang in the branches.
Squirrels scampered up and down the trunk
all day. Two hares ran races round it.
Mice made mousehomes under the roots.
Moles made molehills under the meadow.
Rabbits munched meadow grass in the shade
of the tree.
And at night the owl came, calling
WHOOO WHO WHOOOO?
And they all knew the secret.

Emily, Matthew and Timothy brought sandwiches to eat under the tree. The animals and most of the birds vanished as quick as a wink and watched from hiding places nearby.

The children lay on their backs, drinking lemonade, watching the sun sending sparks through the big floppy leaves. And then they saw the secret too.

In the tree there was a house.

Not a very big house.
Not a very grand house.
Not a house with chimneys and a
rain barrel outside.
But a house made of wood.
A house with a window.
A house with a door as well,
and a ladder made of rope to
climb up and look inside.

They called it 'The Chestnuts'.
It needed quite a lot doing to it of course.
They mended the holes with wood and a hammer
and nails. They swept out the old brown
leaves and feathers and dirt. They found a
piece of corrugated plastic to put on the
roof. They even painted the walls inside.
And when all that was done they brought the
furniture; an orange box, a lamp their
mother had thrown away, and, best of all, an
armchair, very old but comfortable, which
they found discarded in the shed. Tim
wheeled it up the hill in a wheelbarrow.
That was hard work, but not as hard as
climbing up the rope ladder with it.

And then they moved in.
They slept at home each night. But
nearly every day they brought
sandwiches to the house, and played
in the tree. No one else knew the
secret. Except for the birds and
animals, who soon got used to the
children.

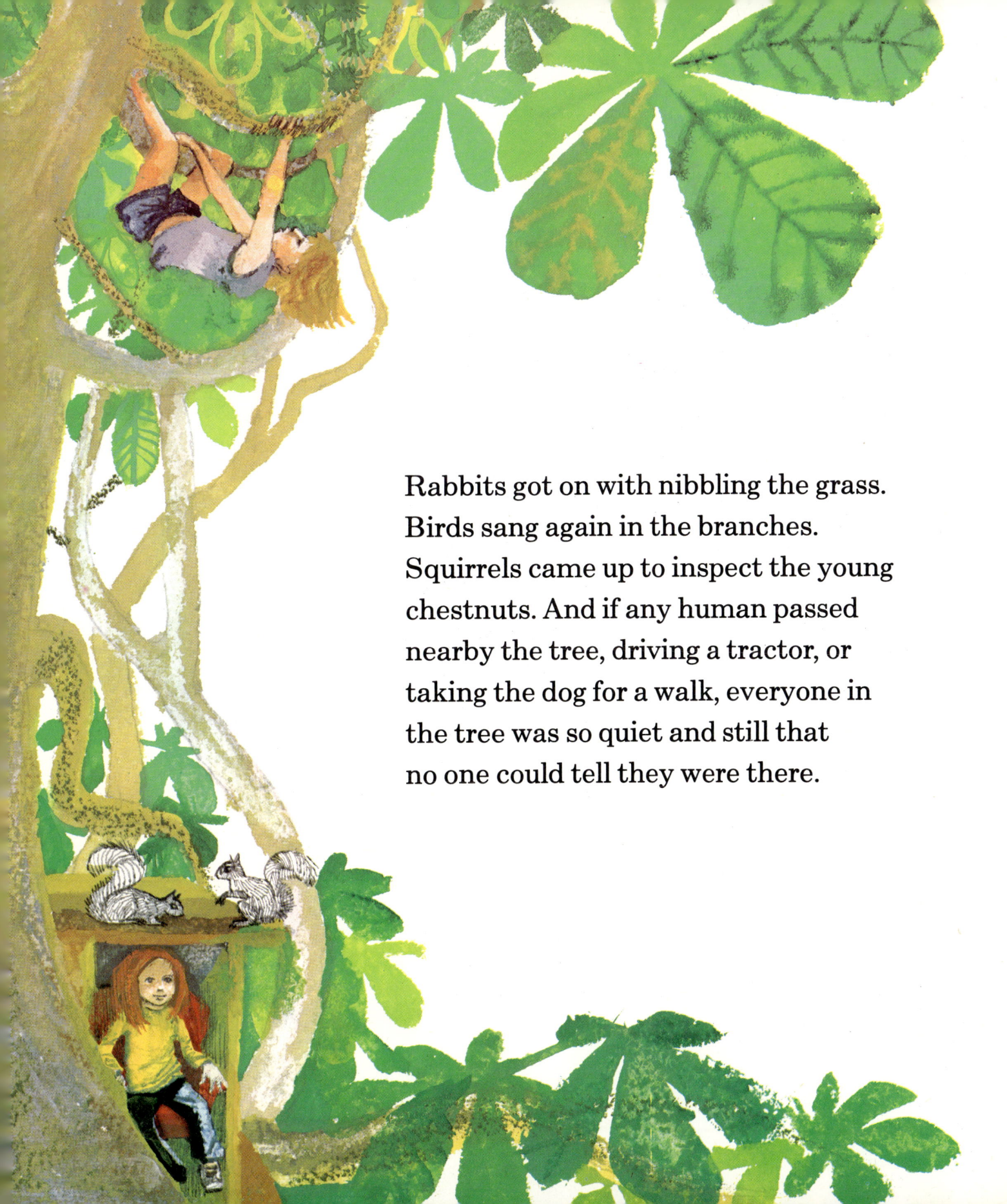

Rabbits got on with nibbling the grass.
Birds sang again in the branches.
Squirrels came up to inspect the young
chestnuts. And if any human passed
nearby the tree, driving a tractor, or
taking the dog for a walk, everyone in
the tree was so quiet and still that
no one could tell they were there.

When the wind blew hard through the leaves and branches Timothy said that he was the Captain of a ship, and Emily and Matthew were his crew. They sailed storm tossed past whales and dolphins. They explored deserted islands. They caught fish or fought pirates all the summer day long.

On other days Emily kept home.
Sometimes she spring-cleaned.
Sometimes she made long lists
of things they needed on a leaf,
and sent the boys out shopping.
On the top branch was a greengrocer's;
lower down ice creams and sweets
were sold. At the foot of the tree
was a baker's.

And there was a butcher shop
by the gateway to the field.

Matthew was King of a castle and a huge
army too. Timothy was his General, and
Emily had to be the princess. She found
it rather boring waiting for the soldiers
to come home from battle, so she disguised
herself as a knight and went with them.
The army had a huge supply of ammunition;
Chestnut cannonballs and arrows made from
twigs. The tree was surrounded by enemies.
Wolves in sheep's clothing and fierce fanged
rabbits. The enemy even had an orange tank
which sometimes roared about in the next
field all day.

One morning in conker time the children got up very early, almost before the sun. They wanted to take breakfast up to the tree.

When they got there Timothy and Emily climbed the ladder and went in first. It was still rather dark inside.

'I think someone has been here,' said Tim.

'Who?' said Emily, sitting down on the comfortable chair.

'Who, whoooooo,' shrieked something rushing past them to the door.

Matthew, who was carefully carrying the sandwiches, nearly got knocked off the ladder,

'What was it?' said Emily, 'Did you
see it? What was it like?'

'It was a monster,' said Tim. 'It
has eyes like headlights, claws like a
tiger, and a red open mouth with sharp
teeth, I think.'

'It was a bird, I think,' said Matthew,
looking over the squashed sandwiches.
'No it wasn't,' said Tim rather loudly.
He still had not got over his fright.
'It was a real live dragon. He lives in the
house at night.'
When they had finished the squashed
sandwiches, and collected the day's conkers,
they went home. And they never came too
early or stayed too late in the tree again.

The days were getting shorter, and the nights were getting longer. Gales of wind snatched the last leaves off the tree. Emily and Tim went back to school. It was too rainy to play outside. The animals had the tree house to themselves again. Birds sheltered inside from the storms. Squirrels hid their nuts in corners. A brave dormouse nested under the cushion of the comfortable chair. Even the owl did not know she was there. Ever since the children had given him such a fright one morning at sunrise, he had been very careful only to come after dark and leave before dawn.

When the Christmas holiday came it snowed. The children had no time to play in the tree. They had other games, like snowballs, or snowman building, or toboganning down the hill. The treehouse was empty. There were a few new holes in it. Part of the roof blew away, and the rope ladder got tangled up in the branches. The squirrels were asleep. The dormouse was fast asleep. All winter long only a few birds, and the owl, were awake to visit the house.

When spring came back, and the big sticky
buds were breaking open to let the leaves
out again, Matthew, Emily and Timothy went
up the hill to look at last year's tree
house. And they found out that the tree
had a new secret. This time it meant that
the children had to stay away for a while.
The owl had brought his wife to the house,
and was busy bringing up a family in what
was left of the comfortable chair.

First published 1974 by
André Deutsch Limited
105 Great Russell Street London WC1

Printed in Great Britain by
Colour Reproductions Limited
Billericay Essex

ISBN 0 233 96575 0